To Owen,

Enjoy the adventures

of Duncan!

This book is dedicated to my parents,
Vincent and Clara Arno, who left a legacy
of family, love, warmth, wisdom, humor,
and delicious food.

Thank you to my son, Eric Bernsen, and all
my family and friends for their support.

Happy Reading

Laura Arno Bernsen

June 16, 2018

www.mascotbooks.com

Bark Once for a Cheeseburger

For more information, please contact:
Mascot Books
560 Herndon Parkway #120
Herndon, VA 20170
info@mascotbooks.com

Library of Congress Control Number: 2017901740

CPSIA Code: PBANG0617A
ISBN-13: 978-1-63177-637-3

Printed in the United States

Bark Once For A Cheeseburger

WRITTEN BY LUCIA ARNO-BERNSEN

ILLUSTRATED BY LAURIE BARROWS

Every summer, Lucy looked forward to riding the ferry from Hyannis to Nantucket Island with her family. When the steamship rounded Brant Point Lighthouse, the island looked the same, but summers were going to change...

Lucy rode her bike
to the penny candy store
where she noticed a sign
that read "Golden Retrievers
for Sale." To save money, Lucy
painted shells and rocks to sell.
She also sat on a bench on
cobblestoned Main Street with
her best friend Sheila to sell
water lilies.

"Hi, would you like to buy some water lilies? They're 25 cents each or six for a dollar," Lucy asked as people walked by.

During the summer, Lucy's family worked at their restaurants every day. When Lucy asked her mom, Clara, for a dog, she smiled but said, "Lucy, we don't have time to care for a dog."

"Please! I promise to take care of it, and I saved all this money. Please!" Lucy pleaded.

After talking about caring for the dog, her mom agreed. Lucy's brown eyes lit up, and she shouted, "Let's go right now!"

Lucy held each of the soft, furry puppies. Mrs. Maynard, the breeder, described their personalities. "All four of the puppies are very different, Lucy. There's Sleepy who loves to nap, Speedy who likes to run, Snuggly who likes to cuddle, and Smarty who loves to eat and figured out how to get free from a rope!"

"I want the smart one who likes to eat because we have lots of restaurant food! I'll name him Duncan like my yo-yo," Lucy said.

Duncan was easy to train because he was so smart and loved the treats Lucy gave him for listening. Her mom, dad, and two brothers loved Duncan so much they had doggie bags made for the restaurants with Duncan's picture on them! When customers couldn't finish their food, they took home the leftovers in Duncan doggie bags.

Duncan grew up to be big and strong, and each summer he waited outside the restaurants to eat. His favorites were cheeseburgers, spaghetti, meatballs, and pizza. When Duncan barked once, Chef Vincent called out, "One cheeseburger coming up for my pal."

He trained Duncan how to order his food. Duncan barked once for a cheeseburger, twice for spaghetti, three times for meatballs, and four times for pizza.

VINCENT'S Restaurant

Duncan's favorite ice cream shop was The Juice Bar, where there was always a long line. Duncan would wait for ice cream to fall out of a cone. Quicker than a cheetah, he would lick it all up from the sidewalk! Sometimes he would walk quietly behind someone eating ice cream and bark loudly to cause it to fall to the ground for him to eat.

At the beach Duncan always wanted to play, but that made Lucy tired and she wanted to lie on her towel to read. He had an idea, and it worked every time. He sat near the edge of the shore with a tennis ball in his mouth. When someone walking on the beach came close, Duncan rolled the tennis ball with his nose to land at the walker's feet.

The strangers would ask, "Hi there, fella. Want me to throw the ball?"

Duncan always wagged his tail wildly and panted as if to say, "Yes, please!"

Duncan fetched the ball until the person moved on. Duncan would then lie down with the wet tennis ball and wait to meet his next new friend.

Duncan was a friendly dog, but sometimes he caused problems. Like a magician, Duncan freed himself from every chain and lock to walk around Nantucket on his own. Maggie, a dog officer, knew Duncan well because she would find him wandering the island alone. She often called Lucy gruffly to say, "I picked Duncan up again today."

One day while Lucy walked Duncan, he escaped his leash and ran away. Maggie found him collecting tennis balls at the tennis courts.

Maggie was upset with Lucy and scolded her to make sure Duncan did not get loose anymore.

Lucy tried a special chain to keep Duncan in the yard, but one day he broke free and wandered to the dock. As Duncan walked toward the wharf, he realized Maggie had seen him.

He didn't want to be caught so he tried to jump on the ferry leaving the harbor, but he was too late! He was a very good swimmer, but the strong waves caused by the boat's engines overcame him. Duncan was starting to drown!

The passengers on the boat all screamed, "Someone help the dog! Please! Help the dog!"

Maggie dove off the pier to save Duncan. When she finally pulled Duncan to shore, she called Lucy who ran to the wharf as fast as she could.

"Duncan! Duncan, we almost lost you there, fella," Maggie said.

"Thank you for saving Duncan. I'm sorry. It's all my fault," Lucy said.

Seeing the fear in Lucy's face, Maggie said, "It's okay, Lucy. I'm not angry at you. I'm just glad we got Duncan in time."

As the family gathered together to celebrate Duncan's birthday, Lucy's mother, Clara, shared her happiness that Lucy convinced her to bring Duncan home. He could not wait to eat his cheeseburger. Everyone knew more adventures were to come from this daring and lovable dog.

ABOUT THE AUTHOR

Lucia Arno-Bernsen lives on Nantucket, and her roots go back to 1954 when her father visited with her two older brothers. Learning there was no Italian food dining, he and her mother pioneered the first Italian Restaurant called Vincent's in 1955. A second restaurant, Arno's, opened in 1960. Lucia spent every summer and several years after college working in the restaurants and writing before moving back to Boston to work in sales and marketing in the cable TV industry.

She is also a freelance feature writer and columnist. She has one grown son and is from Belmont, Massachusetts. *Bark Once for a Cheeseburger* begins a series of children's books sharing the tales of daring and lovable Duncan, her golden retriever.